Barney
The Boat Dog

Runaway Horse!

For Caroline and Barney

First published in the UK in 2011 by Usborne Publishing Ltd., Usborne House,
83-85 Saffron Hill, London EC1N 8RT, England.
www.usborne.com

Copyright © Linda Newbery, 2011
Illustrations © Usborne Publishing Ltd., 2011

Cover illustration by John Butler, johnbutlerart.com
Illustrations by John Francis, courtesy of Bernard Thornton Artists, London

The name Usborne and the devices ♀ 🎈 are Trade Marks of
Usborne Publishing Ltd.

A CIP catalogue record for this book is available from the British Library.

J MAMJJASOND/11 02167/1 ISBN 9781409521990
Printed in Reading, Berkshire, UK.

Barney
The Boat Dog

Runaway Horse!

Linda Newbery

Illustrated by John Francis

USBORNE

Chapter One

Barney and Jim had spent the whole summer exploring the waterways on their narrowboat, *Whistling Jack*. Now it was autumn; the leaves had turned golden and crisp, and were beginning to fall.

Barney loved his life on *Whistling Jack*. He and Jim could go anywhere a river or canal took them. Usually the canals stretched through country fields and woods, but sometimes they'd be next to a railway with trains rushing past, or in a town, where the canal squeezed between high buildings and alongside busy streets. They might pass through a long, lonely stretch of moorland, with hills in the distance and buzzards calling overhead. Sometimes the canal went into a tunnel – Barney would *never* like those – or it was carried high on an aqueduct, across a valley. That felt very peculiar to Barney – like sailing through the sky. Looking down made him feel dizzy, but *Whistling Jack* chugged across the watery bridge as if there was nothing strange about it at all.

Today, Barney knew exactly where they were going. Jim had moored up at Puddleshore, and tomorrow they'd head on up the canal to Steepletown. Steepletown was where Jim's son Peter lived, with his wife Penny and their little boy, Freddie. Jim loved his small grandson, and tried to see the family whenever he could. Barney liked these visits, too; Freddie was full of fun and energy, always playing games of throwing and chasing.

Barney didn't follow *everything* that Jim said to him, but he understood quite a lot. He knew that tomorrow was a special day, and that Jim had been looking forward to it all week. At the canalside town of Puddleshore, Jim went to the baker's shop he always visited when they moored up here, and collected a birthday cake he'd ordered, in the shape of a big seven. Then he went to another shop for candles and a birthday card.

"There! That's everything," Jim told Barney, and they walked back to the boat,

Jim carrying the cake very carefully in its box.

Back on board, Jim made himself a mug of tea, and settled down to finish the model boat he'd spent the last month making. He'd carved it from wood, and now he was finishing the painting and varnishing. It was a model of *Whistling Jack*, a special birthday present for Freddie.

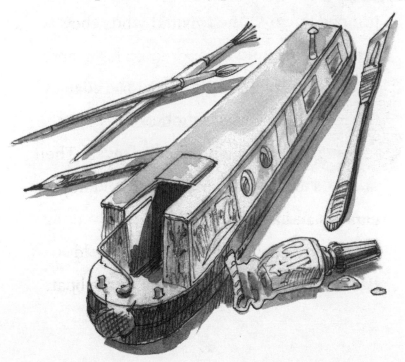

Jim took out his paints, and his finest brush, and began painting the name in careful letters.

It was a sunny evening. The canal bank beckoned, and the light was golden through the leaves. Barney felt too full of energy to settle down and rest, and it wasn't dinner time yet. He gave a little *gruff* to tell Jim he was going ashore, then jumped down to the towpath and set off to see what he could find.

Their mooring-place was at the edge of the town. The bank stretched away invitingly, fringed with reeds. Ducks quacked as Barney trotted past, and another narrowboat chugged slowly along. A big collie standing on its roof thumped its tail at Barney and smiled a greeting, and he whuffed back.

Passing the last of the canalside cottages, Barney came to a paddock with a horse in it – a big, strong horse, black, with a white blaze down its face. Seeing Barney, it came over at a smart trot, and leaned its neck over the fence to snuff at him.

Barney was glad the fence was there. He wasn't sure about horses – he saw them in fields often enough from *Whistling Jack*, but had never been this close to one. It was

so *big*! Its head was larger than the whole of Barney, and its hooves – almost covered by thick fringes of hair – were the size of Jim's dinner plates. It smelled warm and horsey. Below a thick forelock, its eyes were brown and kind, and it snorted at him in a friendly manner.

With a little duck and a yip, Barney showed that he wanted to play. He dashed along the length of the fence, and the horse arched its neck and pranced after him. Soon Barney was through the railings and dashing round the field, with the horse bucking and cantering behind. Round and round in mad circles he raced, till both he and the horse were dizzy and panting.

"Barney!" came Jim's voice from the boat. "Dinner time!"

With a bark of farewell, Barney set off at a run. Just before he reached *Whistling Jack*, he looked behind him and saw the horse standing by its fence, feet squarely planted, head high, eyes watching him.

He knew that the horse wanted him to stay longer, playing their game of chase. It must be lonely, standing in a field with nothing to do but eat grass.

But a few moments later, Barney was gulping down his meat and biscuits, and had forgotten the horse altogether.

Chapter Two

Stretched out on his blanket, on the top
bunk above Jim's, Barney was dreaming.
His whiskers twitched and his paws made
little running movements.

In his dream, the canal stretched long
and wide. Narrowboats plied up and down
in both directions. But there was no engine

sound, no tang of diesel, because all the
boats were pulled by horses – big, strong
horses like the one he'd met in the field.
It might have been a picture from one of
Jim's books: horses plodding along the
towpath, boats gliding behind them.
He heard the ripple of water, and the
boatmen's shouts as they called to each
other and to their horses.

The horse he could see most clearly was black, with a white blaze down its face, and feathery fringes that almost covered its hooves. It stepped out proudly, neck arched. Recognizing his new friend, Barney whuffed, and the horse raised its head to snort a greeting.

Early next morning, Jim was up and dressed early. The first thing he did was open the doors and look outside. It was a bit misty today, and pale cloud hung over the water and the trees, but Jim knew weather, and thought there would be sunshine later.

"Looks like a good day for Freddie's birthday!" he told Barney.

When they'd both had their breakfast, Jim swept *Whistling Jack* from end to end, and polished all the taps and the door handles, and watered the window boxes that stood on the roof.

"Got to look our best," he told Barney. "Special day today!"

Freddie's birthday cake with its candles was hidden in the cupboard, and the model narrowboat, bright in its newly-painted colours, stood on the table, draped in a cloth.

"Right, then," Jim said, when everything was clean and tidy. "Let's get started."

He went to his place at the back of the boat, by the tiller, and Barney jumped up to the roof, where he liked to stand for the best view as they set off. He expected the

engine to throb into life, but nothing happened.

Jim tutted, and turned the key again. Nothing.

Six more tries, and still there was no spark of life. Jim pushed back his cap, and muttered to himself.

"Plenty of fuel! That's not the problem.

Never had this before! It'll be all right in a minute, Barney Boy – you wait and see."

He waited a few moments, then tried again. Still the engine was silent. It refused to give the tiniest sputter or grumble.

"Oh dear, oh dear." Jim was anxious now, and getting hot. What could be wrong? He threw off his jacket, opened the hatch and got down on all fours to see what he could see. Nothing had come loose, no wires springing free. But he remembered now that he should have gone to the boatyard for *Whistling Jack*'s yearly service when they'd passed through Bridgethrupp the month before last. How could he have forgotten?

Now what? He couldn't let Freddie

down – not on his birthday! Freddie would be so disappointed if *Whistling Jack* didn't arrive after all.

Jim tried again. A man from another narrowboat, moored farther down the bank, had seen that something was wrong, and came to help. Between them they tightened bolts and checked wiring.

"Looks like your twin-flanged sparking rod. That'll be your problem," said the other man, nodding wisely.

"Oh," said Jim, looking puzzled. "I thought it might be the ancillary coupling grommet."

"Could be. Could be. Whichever, it doesn't look like you'll be moving on till this is sorted. I'd give you a lift, only I'm heading the other way. There's a mobile mechanic at Withybank. Want me to stop off there – see if he'll drive up here and sort you out?"

"Would you?" Jim asked, brightening.

"Course – oh, no, but it's Saturday. He doesn't work Saturdays. Looks like you're here for the weekend. Good luck, mate."

Jim thanked him for his help, and went

inside. Absent-mindedly, he patted Barney's head, wondering what to do.

He hated the thought of disappointing Freddie, especially today, but he couldn't see how to avoid it. *Whistling Jack* wasn't going anywhere.

Barney was puzzled. He'd been waiting on the roof, expecting the rumble of the engine to vibrate through his paws. Then Jim would unfasten the mooring-ropes and *Whistling Jack* would nose out into the canal. But they were still at their mooring, and Jim had gone into the little kitchen and was making himself a mug of tea.

"Oh dear, oh dear," he was saying to himself. "We're in a fix, that's what we're in."

Barney tried to look helpful. Jim gazed at him, and shook his head sadly. He sat at the table and finished his tea. Then he got up, and put on his coat and cap.

"There must be a bus, Barney!" he said. "We'll go and see if we can find one. If not, I'll have to phone Peter for a lift. It'll be disappointing for Freddie, but it's the best we can do."

He wrapped up the model boat in a tablecloth, and tucked it under his arm. Then he fetched the birthday cake from the cupboard, and held the box by its ribbon ties.

"Come on, boy. We'd best set off now, in case there's a long wait for a bus."

Barney jumped down to the canal bank. Jim locked *Whistling Jack*'s doors and climbed ashore, then began walking along the towpath towards the town.

Instead of following, Barney stood on the path looking in the other direction. Along the bank, close to the fence, was a shape in the mist: a big, dark shape, with pricked ears. It was the horse, watching them. When it saw Barney it gave a small nickering sound.

Barney was reluctant to leave his new friend. He hesitated, looking from the horse to Jim and back again.

Last night's dream floated into his mind.

He had an Idea.

He gruffed at Jim, and hurtled along the path towards the paddock fence.

Chapter Three

It took a few moments for Jim to realize
that Barney wasn't trotting along behind.
He turned round to look.

"Barney?" he called. It wasn't like
Barney to run off, and this wasn't the best
time. He whistled; he called again.
"Barney? Come on, boy!"

Then he saw Barney
on the towpath, some
way off. Barney was
standing still,
looking back at
him, very alert.

Sometimes, Jim
thought, it was almost
as if Barney could speak. This was one of
those times. Quite plainly, Barney was
saying, *Come with me! I've got something to
show you.*

Although Jim was anxious to get into
town and find out what time the bus left,
he walked towards Barney, carefully
carrying the cake and the model boat.

"What is it, boy?"

Barney wriggled and wagged his tail.

Jim saw, in the field, a great strapping horse – a fine creature with strong legs and back and an arched neck. For a moment he thought he was seeing Boxer again. He used to stop here sometimes, years ago, and had chatted to a friendly woman who kept her horse in this paddock. But Boxer had been brown, and this horse was black.

It was reaching out its head to snuff at Barney when a voice called, "Puzzle! Puzzle!" At once the horse raised its head, and cantered towards the voice.

A woman in a red jacket and a patchwork hat was approaching the towpath from a footpath that crossed the next field. She stroked Puzzle's nose and gave him a piece of carrot; then, seeing Jim, she stared.

"Jim? Is that you?"

"Fay!" called Jim. "What, you've got yourself another horse?"

"Yes! It's been three years since dear old Boxer died, and now I've got Puzzle. He needed a good home. He's retired from work, but you wouldn't know it. Is this your little dog? You didn't have a dog last time I saw you."

"That's right," Jim said, smiling proudly. "This is Barney. My best friend, he is."

When she'd patted and admired Barney, Fay went into the shed by the towpath to fetch a bucket of food for Puzzle. Puzzle stuck his nose in, and a fountain of oats sprayed up as he snorted. Soon he was chomping happily.

Jim ventured close enough to pat his neck. Horses were so *big*! And this one was even larger than Boxer had been. He marvelled that Fay was so confident with such big, strong animals.

"Are you moored up for long?" Fay asked.

"Well," said Jim, "I was hoping to be along the canal by now, but I've got a bit of a problem."

"Oh?" said Fay.

Jim explained about Freddie's birthday, and Steepletown, and the cake and the model boat, and the problem with *Whistling Jack*'s engine.

"Puzzle could help out," said Fay. "Why not do it the old-fashioned way?"

"What do you mean?" asked Jim, a bit slow to understand.

"He used to pull a narrowboat, years ago, before he switched to pulling a cart. He's a good old boy. Why don't we harness him to your boat? You've got a tow rope, I suppose?"

Jim thought of all the books he'd read about narrowboats – all the pictures he'd seen of horses plodding the towpath. Before narrowboats had engines, that was the way they moved about.

Wouldn't it be lovely to give Freddie such a surprise – to arrive by horse-power! Oh, yes!

"That's really kind of you – very kind indeed," he told Fay. "Would he really do it? Pull us all the way to Steepletown?"

"No problem for a strong chap like Puzzle," Fay said. "He'll love it. He doesn't get out of the field enough, to be honest – I work such long hours at the hospital. So you'll be doing us both a favour, really, giving him an outing."

"If you're quite sure," Jim said. "The problem is, I'm afraid I'm not terribly good with horses. What if he won't do what I want?"

"Well, listen. I'm off work today – on call. Why don't I come with you? I can bring Puzzle back tonight, and you can stay at Steepletown, and get your boat fixed on Monday."

"*Would* you?" said Jim. "It's very kind of you!"

"It'll be fun! Just like old times, for Puzzle. Let's get him harnessed up."

When Puzzle had finished eating, Fay brought a bridle and a heavy collar out of the hut, and lots more leather straps, and buckled them on. "See," she explained, "this strap goes *here*, and this one loops through *here*, and the buckle fastens like this, and your tow rope ties to this bar, *here*, and then to the front of the boat – easy!"

She led Puzzle through the field gate and out to the towpath, where he stood proudly by *Whistling Jack*, ready for work. He seemed to have made himself taller.

Jim noticed that Barney was looking very pleased with himself, almost as if this was *his* idea.

"Right then! Off we go," said Fay, when she'd checked all the straps and fastenings. She nodded at Jim, who untied the mooring-ropes and climbed on board, with Barney. Fay stayed on the towpath with Puzzle. She made a clicking sound, and told him, "Walk on, boy!"

At once Puzzle stepped forward. He hesitated as he felt the weight of the boat behind him, then leaned into his collar. Slowly and steadily, *Whistling Jack* edged away from the bank, and water rippled alongside.

They were on their way!

Fay walked at Puzzle's head for a few

minutes until he was settled; then she called to Jim to bring *Whistling Jack* close enough to the bank for her to step aboard, joining him and Barney on the rear deck.

"He's a good old boy," she said. "*Walk on*, to start, *Whoa, boy*, to stop – that's all he needs."

"Ah! This is the life," Jim said. "Now, shall we have a cup of tea?"

"That would be—" Fay began, but just

then her mobile phone rang. She snatched it out of her pocket, and listened. "Oh. I see. Yes, all right then. Give me half an hour."

"Something wrong?" asked Jim.

"Yes. I'm sorry! Someone's off sick, and I've got to work after all."

"Oh dear, oh dear," said Jim. "Should we turn back?"

"It's lucky we haven't come far." Fay snapped her mobile shut and slipped it back in her pocket. "Tell you what, though. Puzzle's a sensible chap – he knows his job. You keep going, and I'll get a lift up to Steepletown after work. And I'll give you my phone number in case anything goes wrong. You'll be okay on your own, won't you?"

Chapter Four

It felt strange to Barney to be moving along the canal on a silent boat – no engine noise, no throbbing, no smell of diesel, just the ripple of water and the steady clop of hooves. He stood on the prow of *Whistling Jack*, wagging his tail. He was delighted that things had turned out so well, thanks

to his brilliant idea. When another
narrowboat passed them, going towards
Puddleshore, he heard shouts of
astonishment, and all the people on board
– five of them – came out to stare. It wasn't
every narrowboat that had a fine strong

horse to pull it. Barney felt very proud.

Puzzle walked steadily along the towpath, hooves clinking against stones, tail swishing gently with each step. Then Barney saw his ears flick backwards, and he stopped dead, turning to gaze back the

way they'd come. He seemed to have realized that Fay wasn't with them any more. Without her, he seemed suddenly unsure of himself.

"Walk on! Walk on, good boy!" Jim shouted, and he tried clicking his tongue just as Fay had done. It came out as a startled squeak. Barney whuffed encouragement. Between them, surely they could persuade the horse to carry on walking! But Puzzle stood like a statue, head raised. Next he tried to turn right round.

"No! No!" shouted Jim, but that only made things worse. Puzzle stopped, then ran back. His hind hooves skidded on the mud at the edge of the bank, and one leg slipped right into the water. When he'd scrambled up and got all four hooves firmly on the path, he started to paw at the ground, scraping up stones. The leading-rope looped round his neck had come unfastened, and his front foot landed on it. He tried to toss his head, couldn't lift it, and rolled his eyes in fear.

"Oh dear, oh dear!" Jim muttered. He was having a hard job stopping the back end of *Whistling Jack* from swinging out into the canal, and now another narrowboat was trying to come past.

Puzzle wasn't trying to be difficult, Barney knew. He might be a big, strong horse, but still he could be thrown into a panic. And Jim, not used to horses, didn't know how to calm him. It was up to Barney.

Barney jumped to the bank. Greatly daring, he ran close to the hoof that was planted on the rope, and nuzzled it. Puzzle bent his knee and lifted his foot, and now he could raise his head. The next thing was to get him to walk, and Barney thought he knew how to do that. He ran ahead, turning to Puzzle to whuff at him, reminding him of the game they'd played in the field.

Puzzle lowered his nose, gave two loud snorts, and walked towards Barney. As he leaned into his collar and took the strain, *Whistling Jack* began to move forward again, and the other boat chugged past. Puzzle settled into a steady plod, and Barney gave a sigh of relief. He trotted ahead, tail high.

Everything was under control now! Nothing to it, really. He'd have to keep his wits about him – but then he always did that.

Chapter Five

Jim decided to walk beside Puzzle for a bit. Trying to look as if he did this all the time, he waved cheerily at the man who stood on the rear deck of the other boat.

"Nice horse you've got there," called the other man. "Looks a bit skittish, though!"

"Oh, he's a good boy," Jim called back.

"Just needs a firm hand."

Although he was making himself sound calm, his heart was still pounding after the moments of panic. Puzzle was so big, and so *strong*, and it was hard to know what went on in his head. It was lucky that Barney had been so clever, and had worked out what to do. Now, though, Puzzle was walking steadily along the towpath – and it really wasn't all that far to Steepletown. They had a few lock gates to get through, but they'd easily be there by teatime.

Jim began to enjoy himself. It was lovely to have the boat pulled by a horse in the traditional way. He might have been an illustration in one of the old books he'd read – he felt like a piece of canal history, come back to life. Yes, he could really take to this!

Puzzle snorted, and came to a halt. Jim looked ahead, and saw a new problem. They were coming to a bridge, one of the low curved bridges that crossed the canal, with a farm track over it. *Whistling Jack* could pass underneath it, and so could

Puzzle, but the problem was that there was no towpath on the other side. Beyond the bridge, there was nowhere at all for Puzzle to walk – a post-and-rail fence barred the way, and thick grass, brambles and bushes came right down to the water's edge.

Jim couldn't see what to do. Would he have to unharness Puzzle and find a different way round? But then, if he did that, how would the boat go under the bridge, without a horse to tow it? Jim couldn't pull it, not by himself. He scratched his head in puzzlement.

As they'd stopped, he took the chance to get back on board and go down to the little kitchen, where he took a carrot from the vegetable rack and cut it into pieces. Then he climbed over the side of the boat, went to Puzzle and – more anxious than he wanted the horse to know – held out his hand, flat, with a slice of carrot on it. Puzzle whuffled his whiskery nose towards Jim's hand, took the carrot and crunched it loudly; Jim stroked the horse's smooth cheeks and smelled his warm carroty breath. There! They were proper friends now.

Barney had jumped ashore, too, and was snuffling in the long grass. Then, at a fast scamper, he ran up to the bridge, across, and down the other side. He stopped there, and turned to face Jim, barking. Ah! There *was* a towpath, but it was on the other side of the canal; Puzzle would have to walk up to the bridge, across, down the ramp that pointed back the way they'd come, then

under the bridge along the towpath. The
canals had been built with horses in mind,
so of course there was a way. The bridges
had been made so that a horse could cross
without being unharnessed from its boat.
Jim had seen pictures in books – he tutted
at himself for not remembering.

It would be much easier to do this with two people – one to stay on board, one to lead the horse over and down – but there was only Jim, so he'd have to manage. He released the mooring-rope, and clicked his tongue to Puzzle. "Walk on, boy!"

He must be getting the hang of this. At once Puzzle started to pull, and towed *Whistling Jack* as far as the bridge. He stopped there, uncertain, but Jim took hold of the leading-rope and led the way up and over the bridge, and down. When they reached the towpath, *Whistling Jack* moved forward again.

"Whoa there, boy!" Jim called, confident now. He wanted Puzzle to stop, so that he and Barney could get back on board. But just at that moment, a flight of ducks

rocketed up from the
reeds, with a chorus of
frantic quacking.
Puzzle shot
forward,
snatching the
leading-rope
from Jim's hand,
and surged along
the path as fast as he
could go, with the boat
swaying behind.

Puzzle and *Whistling Jack* were heading
off on their own, with Barney and Jim
stranded on the towpath!

Barney barked; Jim shouted; they both
set off at a run. Luckily Puzzle couldn't
move very fast with the boat holding him

back. Barney, much faster, galloped with
all his strength, ears streaming back, until
he'd overtaken Puzzle – then he lay down
on the path and whuffed at him to stop.
Puzzle, who'd now forgotten the ducks and
couldn't remember why he was in such a
rush, snorted and slowed. The canal was

narrow here, and *Whistling Jack* was just close enough to the bank for Jim to scramble and haul himself aboard.

Phew! Jim whistled to Barney, who jumped across to the side-rail and down to the deck.

"Good boy, Barney," Jim panted, and "Steady there, Puzzle, that's the way!" he called to Puzzle, when he'd got his breath back. "Nice and easy – there's no hurry at all!"

They were all together again, and Steepletown was only a few kilometres off. Nothing else would go wrong now, surely!

Chapter Six

Really, Barney thought as they approached the lock gates, Jim wasn't doing too badly at all. Barney felt quite proud of the way Jim was learning to handle Puzzle, and Puzzle in turn was getting used to Jim. They were becoming a team.

Barney half-expected something to go

wrong as they passed through the lock gates, but everything was fine. Each time Puzzle had to stand and wait while the sluices opened and water gushed and splashed through, Barney sat by his front feet to make sure Puzzle didn't try to move off. Puzzle stood, and tossed his head wisely, and waited for Jim to close the second gate and tell him to walk on again.

They passed through three sets of lock gates. All this took some time, and Barney began to feel hungry. Surely it must be time for lunch? Jim usually stopped at about this time of day, and put the kettle on and got himself something to eat, and Barney had a little something as well.

Sure enough, when they pulled away from the third lock, Jim looked at his watch and said, "I think we all deserve a break, Barney, don't you? Whoa there, boy!" he called to Puzzle, who seemed glad enough to stop too.

Jim moored up, tethered Puzzle by his leading-rope and gave him three more pieces of carrot. Then he went down to the kitchen to cook his lunch. Barney sat close by the stove, watching hungrily. Jim put the kettle on, opened a tin of beans, and took out some bread for toast. Then he dropped a clatter of dog treats into Barney's bowl.

For the next few moments, Barney was too busy eating to notice much. When he'd licked his bowl shining clean, Jim was putting his plate of beans and toast on the table, next to his mug of tea. But instead of sitting down to eat, he said, "Back in a

minute, Barney Boy," and went up the
steps to the foredeck.

Barney ran up after him. On the canal
bank, Puzzle was lying down, stretched out
on his side. Was he ill? Had he collapsed?
Jim and Barney hurried up.

"What's up, old chap?" Jim asked him,
and Barney put his front paws on one of
Puzzle's big knees, and whuffed. Puzzle
raised his head, sighed, and stretched out
again in the afternoon sunshine.

"Oh, I see! You're just having a rest, aren't you, boy?" Jim said, stroking Puzzle's neck. "Well, you've worked hard this morning. Tell you what, I'll take off some of this harness and make you more comfortable. Then you can really relax."

Barney watched while Jim unfastened the buckles and straps and lifted the collar off Puzzle's neck. It looked very complicated, and Barney wasn't at all sure that this was a good idea. He hoped Jim was remembering where everything went, for when he had to put it all on again.

Soon Puzzle was wearing nothing but his bridle, and he stretched out gratefully. Jim laid the collar and the other bits of harness carefully on the grass bank.

"That's better. Now you can have a

proper rest. You deserve it. We'll move on in an hour or so."

Puzzle gave a whuffling snort of contentment, and lay flat out, eyes closed. Jim looked pleased, and went back on board to eat his lunch.

Jim often had a little snooze in the afternoons, too, and when he'd washed up the dishes he went to lie on his bunk. Barney settled by his feet. Within a few minutes, both of them – all *three* of them, counting Puzzle – were sleeping soundly.

Into Barney's mind floated a dream about pigs. His nose twitched to their rich, ripe smell. Their oinking and snuffling filled his head. He scuffled his paws and lifted his ears.

Then he opened his eyes.

No, it wasn't a dream! There were pigs outside – close, very close. He jumped down from the bunk, disturbing Jim, who woke with a muffled "*Whu-uhhh?*"

Wide awake now, Barney ran to the foredeck. Big pink pigs, six of them, were coming down the field beside the canal at a very fast scuttle, snorting and oinking as they ran.

Puzzle was scrambling to his feet. His eyes and nostrils were flared wide. As the pigs scrummed at the fence, as close to him as they could get, he reared in fright, pulling at his rope. Barney jumped to the bank, wondering if he could chase the pigs away, back up their field. He saw their

sharp, clever eyes, their bristly skin, and
their waffling pink noses. They made
cheerful grunting remarks to each other as
they jostled.

This was too much for Puzzle! He pulled
back as hard as he could, and the clip of his
tethering rope snapped away from the
bridle. Realizing he was free, he stood for a
moment unsure – then turned, and set off
at speed, ears flat back.

No! No! Come back!

Barney streaked after him, but Puzzle at
full gallop – and without the boat to slow
him down – was much, much faster.
Barney stopped, and watched in dismay as
Puzzle jumped the low fence into the next

field, and hurtled away up the side of a hill.
Clods of mud and earth flew from his
hooves. Well-rested now, he was full of
energy; he'd already run so far that he
looked like a small toy horse almost flying
over the grass.

"Ohhh – *no!*"

Jim, fully awake now, was standing
on the foredeck of *Whistling Jack*, clutching
the rail in shock. He and Barney gazed at
each other, taking in the full, mind-joggling
awfulness of what had happened.

Chapter Seven

Jim hoped he was dreaming. He blinked several times, hoping he'd wake up and find himself lying peacefully on his bunk.

But he didn't. He wasn't. This was real.

Puzzle had got loose. Galloped away. He was gone.

Jim covered his face with both hands.

What now? How could he tell Fay that her horse was missing? That he'd let Puzzle go, let him career wildly about the countryside?

Barney was dashing to and fro on the towpath, quite plainly saying that they ought to give chase.

"You're right, Barney," said Jim. He hurried back inside to put on his boots – he'd taken them off for his lie-down. Then he locked up, and joined Barney on the bank.

Soon he was puffing up a hill behind Barney, scanning the landscape, looking desperately around for any sign of a large black horse. Jim saw ploughed fields, and woods, and rooks high in the trees; he saw sheep and cows and a tractor, and he even saw the church spire of Steepletown not too far off. But he couldn't see Puzzle.

What if something awful happened? What if Puzzle galloped across a busy road? Jim dizzied himself thinking about it, so tried not to.

Barney was whuffing, nose to the ground, and Jim saw the firm print of hooves, large and round as plates.

"Good boy, Barney," Jim panted.

Through a muddy gateway they went,
following the tracks, to a leaf-scattered
woodland path that wound between trees.
On through a grassy field with cows in it.
The cows were all huddled to one side, as if
a thundering horse had just startled them
– yes, this was the way. Across a stream,
over a rickety bridge, and into a farmyard.

"Was that your horse bolted through
here a little while back?" shouted a
farm-hand. "Tried to catch him, but he was
too quick. He went that way!"

He pointed up an even steeper hill, where a lane sloped up between high hedges. Barney sped on, and Jim stumbled after. He had a stitch in his side now, and had to stop for a moment, doubled up. Then he forced his legs to carry on up the lane.

He couldn't see what was at the top of the hill. He feared seeing a wide-open landscape, stretching out into hazy distance, with no Puzzle to be seen in any of it.

Instead there was a stable-yard – a riding school, with a whole collection of tubby ponies ready to set out, ridden by children. A plump woman was going round from one to another, checking girths and stirrups and hard hats.

Jim was so breathless now that he could hardly speak. "Have you – seen a big – big black – big black horse?" he puffed.

"Yes! Yes, I have," said the woman. "That's Puzzle, isn't it? I was expecting Fay to come looking for him." She looked curiously at Jim and Barney. Jim explained that he was Fay's friend, and that he'd borrowed Puzzle but had got into a bit of trouble. The woman was too busy with her ponies to ask questions, so she just nodded and said, "Don't worry. He's in the paddock there with our old donkey, Esmeralda. He was talking to her over the gate, so I let him in."

Oh! The *relief!* Jim thought his legs would give way. He could almost have burst into tears.

"*Thank you!* Thank you a hundred times!"

"No problem," said the woman. "Just let yourself out when you're ready."

Jim went to the paddock gate and held out a piece of carrot from his pocket. Puzzle whickered at him like an old friend, and came over. The old grey donkey followed, so Jim gave her a piece of carrot too.

It was a bit tricky getting Puzzle through the gate without Esmeralda coming as well, but Barney helped by planting himself in the gateway and barking a *No!* at her.

As Jim led Puzzle through the throng of ponies, he looked back and saw the donkey standing close by the gate. She let out a loud *Orr-ee-orr-ee-orr* as Puzzle walked away, and Puzzle stopped and turned his head before walking obediently next to Jim. Esmeralda looked lonely, standing in the paddock by herself. Still, she had all those ponies for company, so surely she

wouldn't miss Puzzle? She'd be fine. *Everything* was fine, now that Puzzle had been recaptured.

Jim whistled to himself as they set off down the lane – the three of them, together again.

Chapter Eight

If Barney could have said *I told you so*, he'd
say it now. They were back at the canalside,
and Jim had led Puzzle quite confidently all
the way to *Whistling Jack*, but Jim's next
task was to get all the harness back on. He
looked at all the bits and pieces laid out on
the bank and tried to work out how to fit it.

"Now, what did Fay do? She put this bit on first, I'm sure. Or no, was it this? And where does *that* go?"

Barney settled down for a long wait, nose on paws. At last Jim remembered that some of the canal books on his shelf showed pictures of horses in harness, so he fetched one of those. That made it easier, and soon Puzzle was wearing his collar, girth and crupper (Jim had a few problems with that, fitting it over his tail) and the tow rope was firmly attached to *Whistling*

Jack. They were ready for the final stage of their journey!

So easy it seemed now – Puzzle walking steadily, Jim calling encouragement, Barney riding on the roof or running alongside. Soon they'd reached the edge of Steepletown, the cottages with gardens that ran down to the canal, and the first shops.

"They'll be waiting for us," Jim told Barney. "Try to look as if we do this all the time. Show them we're enjoying ourselves. I want to give them a really big surprise."

Barney soon found a way to do that when they reached some steps leading up to a garden gate. Barney ran up, and jumped from the top step to Puzzle's broad back; he wobbled, got his balance, and sat there wagging his tail. Puzzle didn't seem to mind at all. Barney had never ridden a horse before, and decided that he liked it – he got a good view from up here.

On the grass by the bridge, five people were waiting with a picnic – Peter, Penny, Freddie, and two of Freddie's friends who'd been invited for birthday tea. Already Barney could hear their shouts of astonishment. The boys ran down the steps, and Freddie sprinted along the towpath to get to *Whistling Jack* before anyone else. Jim climbed ashore, and there was a lot of hugging, and excitement, and taking of photographs, and explaining. First Freddie and then the others wanted to try steering the boat, while Puzzle pulled, so Jim did a special little trip up the canal and back again, with the boys taking turns at the tiller. Jim felt quite an expert now, showing them how a click of his tongue would tell Puzzle to walk forward, and a *Whoa, boy* would make him stop.

"This is the *best* birthday I've ever had!"
said Freddie. "Shall we play cricket now?"

"Wait, I nearly forgot!" Jim exclaimed.
"You haven't had your present yet, or the
special cake!"

There was a little ceremony of the unveiling of the model boat. Freddie was delighted. He examined it in every detail. "It's *Whistling Jack* exactly! Now I can have *Whistling Jack* at home with me!"

Later, when Jim had taken off Puzzle's harness and tethered him on the towpath for a rest, and the candles had been lit and blown out, and the cake cut up and most of it eaten, Fay arrived to check that everything was all right. Everyone was inside *Whistling Jack* now; dusk was falling, and Freddie's dad was teaching everyone how to play a noisy card game. Jim introduced Fay, and Penny cut her a piece of cake.

"How did you get on?" Fay asked Jim, squeezing in on the sofa-bench, next to

Penny. "Any problems?"

Jim paused; Barney waited, thumping his tail. Then Jim said, "No, not at all! Really nothing worth mentioning. We got on just fine, me and Barney and Puzzle."

Chapter Nine

A month later, on a still autumn afternoon, Jim and Barney were travelling the same stretch of canal. *Whistling Jack*'s engine was running smoothly now, and they had no need of Puzzle's pulling power. But as they neared Puddleshore, Barney stood on the prow, looking forward eagerly. Would he see Puzzle again?

Yes, he would! Jim had phoned Fay to say they were nearby, and Fay said she'd just have time to come and see them before going off to the hospital for her evening shift. Jim had made one of his special carrot cakes as a present for Fay, and had iced a picture of Puzzle on top. And of course he'd saved some carrots for Puzzle.

Jim moored up in the same place as before. At once, Barney jumped ashore, and ran along the towpath, barking. He could already see Puzzle, standing by the fence – even bigger than Barney remembered. There was Fay, in her patchwork hat. She was grooming Puzzle, standing on an upturned box to reach up and brush his mane.

Barney barked a hello, and Puzzle gave a nickering neigh of welcome.

Then there was another sound from behind him. A sort of gasping sound that wound itself up, then bellowed and creaked: *Orrr-eee-orrr-eee-orrr!*

Astonished, Barney skidded to a halt. Behind Puzzle he saw the long, hairy ears of a donkey, and its pale nose. The donkey stepped forward; brown eyes gazed at him.

"Oh! Isn't that Esmeralda?" said Jim.

Fay got down from the box she'd been standing on.

"A*ha*! You didn't tell me you'd met Esmeralda, did you? About Puzzle getting loose and bolting up the hill? About meeting Sue at the riding school?"

Jim went red. "I didn't want to worry

you. And I felt bad about it."

"You needn't feel bad," Fay said, "because it worked out brilliantly. Sue's a friend of mine. She told me what happened, and how Puzzle had palled up with Esmeralda. Then we both had an idea! Esmeralda's an old donkey, retired years ago, and Sue doesn't really need her but wants her to have a comfortable old age. Puzzle was a bit lonely in the field on his own, so it was the obvious answer for Esmeralda to come and live here and be Puzzle's friend."

Barney had listened attentively to all this. He didn't understand *all* of it, but he did understand *some*. And he could see for himself how happy Puzzle looked. Barney thumped his tail, and Puzzle leaned over Esmeralda to snuff at him.

"Well, that's good! Everyone needs a
friend," said Jim, sharing the bits of cut-up
carrot between Puzzle and Esmeralda.
Then he remembered the cake, and went
back to the boat to fetch it. Fay was

delighted, and said that they should each have a piece now, so Jim invited her on board for a cup of tea before she set off for work.

Later, as dusk fell, *Whistling Jack* pulled away, with Jim waving from the tiller and Barney on the roof, thumping his tail. Barney knew he'd see Puzzle, Esmeralda and Fay again before long; Freddie too, and Peter and Penny. It was like that on the waterways. They had lots of friends, good friends, in many different stopping-places.

But, for now, it was just him, and Jim, and *Whistling Jack*, and whatever adventure waited for them next.

Don't miss out on the adventures of Barney the Boat Dog:

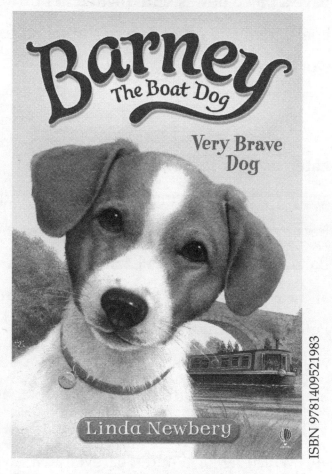

Barney

The Boat Dog

Very Brave Dog

Linda Newbery

ISBN 9781409521983

Barney doesn't like tunnels. They're very scary. But when he gets separated from Jim, Barney has to be brave and face a long tunnel all on his own!

Cat Tales

Curl up with Cat Tales, also by
award-winning storyteller
Linda Newbery. Look out for:

The Cat with Two Names

Two of everything leads to double trouble for Cat...

ISBN 9780746096147

Rain Cat

Is the mysterious cat really controlling the weather?

ISBN 9780746097281

Smoke Cat

Where do the shadowy cats in next door's garden come from?

ISBN 9780746097298

Shop Cat

Strange things have been happening since Twister arrived...

ISBN 9780746097304

The Cat who Wasn't There

Who is the little white cat in Vincent's garden?

ISBN 9780746097328

Ice Cat

A cat made of snow and ice can't come to life...or can it?

ISBN 9780746097311

For more fun and furry
animal stories visit

www.fiction.usborne.com